DEATH

COMING

UP THE

HILL

A NOVEL BY
CHRIS CROWE

Houghton Mifflin Harcourt

Boston • New York

hmhco.com

The text was set in Minion.

The Library of Congress has cataloged the hardcover edition as follows:
Crowe, Chris.
Death coming up the hill / Chris Crowe.
pages cm
Summary: Ashe Douglas keeps a weekly record of historical and personal events in
1968, the year he turns seventeen, including the escalating war in Vietnam; assassina-
tions, rampant racism, and rioting; his first girlfriend; his parents' separation; and a
longed-for sister.
[1. Novels in verse. 2. Coming of age—Fiction. 3. Vietnam War, 1961–1975—Fiction.
4. Social change—Fiction. 5. Family problems—Fiction. 6. Dating (Social customs)—
Fiction. 7. United States—History—1961–1969—Fiction.] I. Title.
PZ7.5.C79De 2014
[Fic]—dc23
2013042812

ISBN: 978-0-544-30215-0 hardcover
ISBN: 978-1-328-90410-2 paperback

Printed in the United States of America
DOC 10 9 8 7 6 5 4 3 2 1
4500710774

976

for the 16,592

in 1968

There's something tidy
in seventeen syllables,
a haiku neatness

that leaves craters of
meaning between the lines but
still communicates

what matters most. I
don't have the time or the space
to write more, so I'll

write what needs to be
remembered and leave it to
you to fill in the

gaps if you feel like
it. In 1968,
sixteen thousand five

hundred ninety-two
American soldiers died
in Vietnam, and

I'm dedicating
one syllable to each soul
as I record my

own losses suffered
in 1968, a
year like no other.

The trouble started
on New Year's Eve when Mom came
home late. Way too late.

Worry about Mom —
and about Dad — knotted my
gut while Dad paced the

living room like a
panther ready to pounce. "Where
the hell is she, Ashe?

Those damn activists . . .
I shouldn't have let her go.
Well, that's the last time,

the absolute last
time she mixes with trouble-
makers. It ends now!"

He looked at me like
it was somehow *my* fault, but
I knew better. He

had to blame someone,
and I became an easy
target. But it made

me angry at him —
and at Mom, too. Why couldn't
they just get along?

What I wished for the
new year was peace at home, in
Vietnam, and the

world. A normal life.
Was that too much to ask for?
The door creaked open,

Mom stepped in, and Dad
pounced. I crept up the stairs, closed
my door, and tuned out.

★ ★ ★

Later, Mom tapped on
my door and came in, timid
as a new kid late

to school. And she smiled
even though she'd just had a
knock-down, drag-out with

Dad. There was a light
in her that I hadn't seen
in a long, long time.

She wanted to check
on me, to make sure I was
okay, to tell me

that May 17,
1951, was the
best day of her life

because it was the
day I was born, and even
though things had been rough,

she had no regrets.
Not one. Then she hugged me and
whispered that maybe,

just maybe, there was
light at the end of this dark
tunnel. "You never

know what's coming up
the hill," she said, then left me
alone, worrying.

Even though he won't
admit it, I blew up my
dad's football career.

They say he had a
future in the NFL,
but his senior year

at the U of A
he quit football because he
got my mom pregnant.

Mom's parents disowned
her, and to them, she and I
no longer exist.

She has a scrapbook
filled with photos and clippings
of Dad when he played

defensive back for

the Arizona Wildcats,

and my favorite

action photo shows

him leaping and reaching for

an interception.

The camera had caught

him right when he snagged the ball.

His head's back, and you

can't see his face, but

you can see his taut forearms

knotted with muscle

and the big number

seventeen on his jersey.

Even as a kid,

I recognized the

strength and grace in that picture,

and I knew he'd been

special, talented,
and I made up my mind to
be like him one day.

Maybe I'd never
be as good as he was, but
I thought that if I

worked hard and became
a great athlete, somehow that
would make up for his

loss. It turned out I
was wrong. I never had to
prove anything to

Dad. His love for me
was as sure and solid as
the U.S. Marines.

Too bad he didn't
feel that way about Mom. He
resented her for

the mistake that killed
his football career, the same
mistake that forced him

to marry her. Back
in 1950, things worked
that way: if a guy

knocked up a girl, he
married her to make it right.
It doesn't happen

like that nowadays.
It's 1968, and
young people believe

in free love, and there
are plenty of ways to take
care of a mistake.

By getting married,
Mom and Dad did the right thing,
and they have been good

parents to me, and
I'm grateful to them both for
putting up with each

other for my sake.
I wish there was some way I
could make it right, make

them right, but ending
the long, cold war between them
was as likely as

a black man being
elected president of
the United States.

It's not going to
happen, but, man, wouldn't it
be great if it did?

Mr. Ruby, my
U.S. history teacher,
wrote a number on

the board to begin
every class. Today it was
"two hundred eighteen."

His gray hair was slicked
back, like always, and his shirt-
sleeves were rolled up, like

always. The faded
Marine tattoo inside his
wrist showed while he wrote

on the board. Then he
asked, "What's the significance
of this number?" I

didn't respond, but
I knew exactly what it
meant. I read the news.

Every Thursday, *The*
Phoenix Gazette reported
the casualties

from the previous
week. But nobody in class
knew that. They guessed all

kinds of dumb answers,
and no one even came close.
They don't like thinking

about dead soldiers
in Vietnam; neither did
I, but I couldn't

help looking for that
news article every week
and skimming it for

the casualty
report. Usually it's
just numbers, but if

some guy from Tempe
or Mesa or Phoenix was
killed, they'll mention his

name and maybe print
a photo of him dressed in
his uniform and

staring like he's dead
serious. Well, now he's just
dead. Looking into

his steely gaze made
me feel hollow, sick, and sad.
I looked anyway.

Things mellowed out at
home. Motorola kept Dad
busy, and Mom stopped

attending rallies
at ASU. She's not a
hippie or some kind

of freak, she just feels
too much. What's going on in
Vietnam sickens

her, and what's going
on in America makes
her sick, too. Well, it

doesn't really make
her sick, it makes her *mad*. And
when she's mad, she's got

to do something, and
back then, that something had been
attending protest

rallies in Phoenix
or over at ASU.
Most nights she was gone,

and that really burned
Dad and ignited a war
at home. I learned how

to navigate the
no man's land between them, but
then for some reason

their tactics changed, and
instead of battling, they
ignored each other.

Something on New Year's
Eve changed Mom; she seemed to have
finally found peace.

★ ★ ★

How does a guy deal
with being torn between two
people he loves? I

knew I was lucky
that I hadn't had to choose
between Mom and Dad.

They're opposites thrown
together because of me,
and they had managed

to keep a shaky
truce for so many years. But
it was difficult.

My dad was a flag-
waving hawk who thought it was
every red-blooded

man's duty to spill
that blood when America
called on him for it.

Mom's an anti-war
dove who gave me a "Hell no,
I won't go!" tee shirt

for Christmas, and she'd
convinced Dad and me that I
had to enroll at

ASU as soon
as I finished high school. "The
student deferment

will keep you out of
the draft," she said, "and unless
we're really stupid,

this war will be done
by the time you graduate."
Dad didn't mind the

deferment. "You can
join the ROTC and
graduate as an

officer," he said.
"The Army needs smart leaders
who can help put an

end to the spread of
Communism over in
Vietnam." But when

I thought about the
four hundred seventy-one
guys who died last week,

I knew I'd go to
college to *avoid* the war,
not prepare for it.

I just hoped the war
ended before I had to
decide, because Dad

didn't need any
more ammunition to use
against my mother.

Everybody was
talking about the new team
coming to Phoenix.

At supper, Dad looked
over the newspaper and
said, "Pro basketball

in the desert?" He
shook his head. "It'll be a
huge waste of money.

Phoenix will never
have the market to sustain
an NBA team.

Besides, basketball's
a black man's game, and we don't
need to go out of

our way to attract
more of *them* to the valley.
It's already bad

enough with all the
Mexicans we've got to put
up with around here."

Mom stood up and left
without finishing supper
or saying a word.

Dad put the paper
down and sighed. "I am tired of
your mother's protests."

★ ★ ★

Mom has always been
sensitive, smart, and involved.
She cries when she reads

about the deaths in
Vietnam, and the racist
murders in the South,

and anything else
that shows people at their worst.
She liked to tell me,

"The Beatles are right,
Ashe: all you need is love." When
she'd say that, Mom looked

a starving kind of
lonely. I knew she meant that
America and

the rest of the world
would be better off if love
somehow trumped hatred,

but I also knew
she wanted love for herself.
Even though she lived

with me and Dad, she
was lonely, and no amount
of activism

could fill the awful
emptiness that made her yearn
for true, lasting love.

Mr. Ruby pinned
a newspaper photo on
the bulletin board.

It wasn't a stock
picture of atrocities:
no naked corpses

littered the jungle
floor, no burned-out huts smoldered
with napalm. No dead

bodies were in sight,
but it was a scene of death
caught right in the act.

A Vietnamese
police chief stood with his back
to the camera;

his right arm was raised,
holding a pistol inches
from a skinny kid's

head. The kid wore a
baggy plaid shirt, and his hands
were tied behind his

back. The cop looked as
quiet as the empty street
behind them, and the

fog of war cast a
haze over the buildings in
the background. The kid's

eyes were closed, and the
side of his head looked flattened,
as if a sudden

burst of air had smacked
him. Though I couldn't see the
bullet, I knew I

was witnessing an
execution in Saigon.
In the photograph

a Vietnamese
soldier looked on, smiling. The
looks of anguish, joy,

and businesslike death
in that photo made me feel
sick to my stomach.

★ ★ ★

Nothing good lasted
at home. Mom attended an
anti-war rally

again, and Dad flipped
out. Even upstairs in my
hideout, I could hear

the yelling. But last
night was different. Mom used
to stand up to Dad,

to throw it right back
at him, but the only voice
I heard was Dad's, and

he was really cranked.
There'd be a lull in his storm,
and I'd listen for

Mom to shout back, but
nothing. I heard nothing. A
terrifying thought

seized me. Had he hit
her? Was she hurt? In the past,
nothing could silence

Mom. I crept to my
door, listening and waiting.
And then Dad's roaring

returned, and I felt
a weird kind of relief. Not
because of his rage,

but because it meant
that Mom was okay. I mean,
even Dad wouldn't

scream at someone who's
unconscious. Mom was still there,
I knew that, but she

wasn't fighting back,
at least not the way she used
to. Something *had* changed.

I was six years old
when I realized that my
parents didn't love

each other. Dad and
I were playing catch in the
backyard, and Mom sat

on the patio
reading a book. It took a
little while to get

the hang of it, but
pretty soon I caught every
ball Dad tossed to me.

"That's my boy," he said,
and patted my head. I leapt
into his arms, like

a puppy, and he
hugged me. While in his embrace
I pleaded, "Mom, come

on!" She must have seen
my eagerness, so she set
her book down and stood

next to us. I looped
one arm around Dad's neck and
reached my other arm

around Mom's. Feeling
their love for me, I tugged to
pull them closer, to

knit us into a
tight group hug, but Dad leaned right
and Mom leaned left, and

I spanned the distance
between them like a bombed-out
bridge. The love I had

felt fell into the
gulf between them, and I knew
they loved me, but not

each other. That's a
crummy thing to learn when you're
only six years old.

* ★ ★

So I grew up in
divided territory,
a home with clearly

defined boundaries
that my parents rarely crossed.
Most of the time we

lived under a cease-
fire interrupted by
occasional flare-

ups. Sadly, the key
members of my family
couldn't hold

together, so my
heart was torn, equal shares of
love for Mom and Dad.

On the board, Mr.
Ruby had "Orangeburg, South
Carolina" and

had written below
that: "3: 17, 18,
and 19." I knew

those weren't the weekly
Vietnam casualties,
but they had to be

important somehow.
What happened in Orangeburg?
That night, I went to

the Tempe Public
Library to see what I
could find about it.

★ ★ ★

The library was
quiet when I entered, and
the librarian

shot me a look that
said I better make sure it
stayed that way. Nodding,

I headed to the
newspaper shelf that had a
couple weeks' worth of

The New York Times in
tidy stacks and started to
go through them. It took

a while, but I found
a small article about
a riot started

by some Negro kids
because they weren't allowed in
a segregated

bowling alley. They
commenced making trouble, and
when the cops showed up,

the mob threw rocks and
bricks, and those Southern police
don't put up with that

stuff, especially
from Negroes, so they started
shooting people. When

it was all over,
twenty-eight people were hurt
and three people were

dead: eighteen-year-old
Samuel Hammond, Jr.;
a nineteen-year-old

kid by the name of
Henry Ezekial Smith;
and a boy about

my age, Delano
Herman Middleton, who was
only seventeen.

I set the paper
down and wondered what could make
a bunch of people

mad enough to start
rioting when they knew the
streets were patrolled by

trigger-happy cops
looking for an excuse to
punish protestors.

Blacks had it lousy,
especially in the South,
but did they really

think a riot would
make things better? Buried deep
in the *Times,* like it

didn't matter, the

story made me realize

Vietnam wasn't

the only place where

Americans were getting

killed. It's happening

here at home, too, but

no one is counting the ghosts

sprouting on our soil.

To Dad, the news was
 like church, and Walter Cronkite
was its pastor. But

after last Tuesday's
special report, Dad stared at
the TV. "I'll be

a son of a bitch,"
he said over and over.
Surprise and anger

rocked him, but Mom looked
jubilant. Smiling like she'd
won a victory,

she stood up, winked at
me, and went to the kitchen
to finish cleaning

up while Dad sat stunned
by Cronkite's betrayal of
America. I

agreed when Cronkite
said we should leave Vietnam,
"not as victors, but

as honorable
people who lived up to their
promise to defend

democracy, and
did the best they could." He was
right. It was time for

us to end the war.
How many had already
died? How many more

would die if we kept
fighting? How much more blood would
it take to conquer

a Southeast Asian
country on the other side
of the world? If the

war didn't end soon,
would my own blood help pay the
price of Vietnam?

A new girl showed up
in Mr. Ruby's class. Tall,
with straight blond hair that

hung past her shoulders —
and gorgeous without trying.
White peace signs and doves

covered her tie-dyed
tee shirt, and while our teacher
signed her admit slip,

she looked around the
room like she owned the place. No
shyness. No fear. Just

confidence. Plenty
of confidence. When Mr.
Ruby finished, he

handed her the slip
and pointed at me. "Take that
desk behind Ashe." My

heart thumped when she walked
down the row and took her seat.
I'd never seen a

high school girl like her.
She looked like a goddess, a
tall, beautiful blond

goddess. I wanted
to turn around and talk to
her, to look at her,

but Mr. Ruby
must have read my mind. "Ashe, you'll
get to know your new

classmate later, but
now you need to focus on
history, okay?"

And then he started
writing on the chalkboard. But
all I remember

from that class is the
stunning look of the new girl,
her perfume, and my

hunger to find out
why I felt like a magnet
attracted to steel.

★ ★ ★

Angela Turner
was the girl's name, and she was
from Los Angeles,

"L.A.," she called it.
Like me, she was the only
kid at home; unlike

me, she wasn't her
family's only offspring.
She had a brother

in Vietnam. When
I heard that, I felt ashamed
by the "Hell no, I

won't go" tee shirt I
had worn to school that day, but
then I remembered

that she was dressed like
a hippie, and it surprised
me that she would be

anti-war with a
brother stuck in Vietnam.
The newspapers can't

print everything, but
I could read between the lines,
and I'd seen enough

news clips and photos
to know it was absolute
hell, hell on earth. If

I had a brother
in Vietnam, what would I
do? Probably I

would oppose the war
but support him as much as
I possibly could.

Unfortunately,
I didn't have a brother
or sister to think

about. I never
had anyone share my room,
my parents, my life.

I grew up in a
house that was quiet as a
graveyard, except for

the occasional
explosions that ripped through our
lives without warning.

Mr. Ruby's eyes
turned red and watery when
he told us about

the Tet Offensive.
"They caught us by surprise, and
we've lost too many" —

his voice trembled, and
we all listened, dead silent,
while he took a deep

breath and continued —
"far too many of our boys
there." The sorrow on

his face and in his
voice paralyzed everyone.
He looked down at the

floor while, spellbound by
his emotion, we waited
for what would come next.

He started crying.
Standing in front of us with
tears streaming down his

cheeks, Mr. Ruby
looked around, his eyes burning
into us. "It's a

shame, you know, a damn
shame that we're in a stupid
war that has led to

senseless suffering
for the civilians and the
soldiers on both sides."

Then he went silent,
head down, arms at his side, and
wept like an old man.

The tension in the
room made us all prisoners
of Mr. Ruby's

anguish. No one moved.
No one laughed. No one knew what
to do. Suddenly

Angela rushed by
me and went to our teacher.
Gently turning his

back to the class, she
wrapped her long arms around him
and held him while his

shoulders shook. Then she
looked at me, looked at all of
us petrified with

stupidity. "You
all should leave now. Let the man
have some privacy."

Some kids bolted for
the door, and the stress bled out
of the room like air

from a balloon. I
stayed in my seat, watching the
new girl from L.A.

giving comfort to
a man who was both teacher
and stranger to her.

I ached to know what
it would feel like to have her
long arms around me.

The bodies piled up
over there. Hundreds every
week, with thousands more

wounded. And we had
problems at home. Race riots
last year were caused by

discrimination
that still lingered. Anti-war
rallies stirred people

up, too, and sometimes
it felt like America
was ready to blow.

I was in the midst
of a different war at
home. No one lobbed live

hand grenades or shot
guns, because our conflict was
a war of silence,

not violence. The
demilitarized zone was
up in my bedroom,

where I went to tune
out and where my parents came
to check on me. They

didn't want me to
be a victim of their war,
but it was too late.

They never came in
together. Instead, it was
a tag-team mission:

Dad walked in, turned off
my stereo, and sat on
my bed like an old

friend. He'd tell me how
integrated circuits were
going to transform

the electronics
industry. I pretended
to listen, but I

was thinking that he
should instead talk about how
another kind of

integration might
transform America. When
it was Mom's turn, she

talked about all the
stuff she'd done to end the war
in Vietnam. But

I told her that I
wished she'd try to end the war
with Dad instead. She

listened, I had to
give her that; then a sad smile
darkened her face, and

she sighed. "I'm afraid
it's too late for that, Ashe. Your
father and I got

married because of
you, and we're still together
because we love you,

and that's probably
the best we can do." Then her
smile faded, and my

heart sank. "I'm not sure
how long we're going to last."
She looked ready to

confide something but
paused and asked, "You understand
what's going on, right?"

Angela Turner
stopped me after class today.
We stood outside the

classroom door, unmoved
by students streaming around
us, and talked about

Mr. Ruby's class
and Vietnam, civil rights,
and Martin Luther

King, her hero. She
told me about her brother
and her parents, and

herself. "Mom and Dad
adopted me when I was
a baby and saved

me from who knows what
kinds of crap I would have dealt
with in the foster

care merry-go-round."
She looked at me, hard, like she
was trying to read

my mind. The bell rang
and the hallway emptied, but
neither one of us

moved. She leaned closer —
so close I breathed in her peach
perfume — and said, "So

my real parents dumped
me." Her eyes stayed on mine, and
I didn't know what

she wanted me to
say or do. Finally I
shrugged and said, "So what?"

Her glistening lips
formed a smile. "That is a good
question, Ashe, the right

question." For a few
awkward moments no words passed
between us, and my

heart thudded so hard
I was afraid she'd hear it.
"Someone said there's a

Sadie Hawkins dance
in two weeks. Are you going?"
"Haven't been asked," I

replied. Then her smile
widened, brightened, and she said,
"What about going

with me?" A wave of
heat flowed up my neck, and I
felt my face redden.

"I'd really like that."
Her eyes narrowed, and with a
nod she said, "A good

answer, Ashe. The right
answer," and turned and walked to
her next class. As I

watched her leave, I tried
not to think about what Dad
would do if he found

out I was going
to a dance with a gorgeous
hippie from L.A.

Thursday night, I asked
Dad to take us to Coco's
for dinner. "You know,

like a regular
family?" He rolled his eyes but
agreed. We sat in

a booth near the bar.
An old black-and-white TV
in the corner had

the news on, talking
about LBJ's speech last
Sunday, when he said

he would try to get
us out of Vietnam and
that he wouldn't run

for reelection.
Mom looked nervous, happy, and
pretty, and when she

talked to Dad, he paid
attention. They looked just like
a couple on their

first date: awkward but
interested. I'd never
seen them like that, and

it seemed almost too
good to be true. By the time
the waiter brought my

chocolate shake for
dessert, it looked like Mom and
Dad were softening

up. After shooting
me an awkward smile, Mom looked
at Dad. "Ashe is the

best thing about us,
and we owe it to him to
solve this, no matter

what might be coming
up the hill. He deserves a
better future than

we had." Dad nodded
slowly, but before he could
speak, a commotion

interrupted him.
Someone turned up the TV
at the bar, and we

all turned to watch a
grim-faced reporter clutching
his microphone. "The

Reverend Martin
Luther King, Jr., has been
gunned down outside a

Memphis motel. He's
in critical condition . . ."
A hush fell over

the room, and Mom went
pale white and shaky, but that
changed when some guy at

the bar yelled, "About
time!" His buddies burst into
wild laughter, and Mom's

face turned furious
red. When Dad started laughing,
too, he dropped a bomb

on our night out. Mom
stood, fierce blue eyes blazing. "Come
on, Ashe, we're done here."

As a kid, I dreamed
of becoming a hero.
War movies had taught

me that the hero
saved his buddies by diving
on a live grenade,

so in our childhood
war games I always played that
guy. Someday, I thought,

my valor would earn
me a Medal of Honor.
Things changed when I got

older and learned that
real war is nothing like the
movies. I started

wondering if I
had what it took to be a
hero. Would I have

the guts to cover
a live grenade for my friends?
Would I sacrifice

my life for someone
else? Sometimes that's exactly
what a guy doesn't

want to learn about
himself. The thing is, there are
all kinds of grenades

in life; you don't have
to go to Vietnam to
find them. I knew that.

APRIL 1968

Martin Luther King's
murder knocked the wind out of
Angela. She missed

a few days of school
right after, and when she came
back, she looked like she

might break if she sat
down too hard. Mr. Ruby
welcomed her to class

with a nod, and she
slid into her desk behind
me, leaned forward, and

whispered, "Ashe, I hate
what happened to him, but those
riots in D.C.

and everywhere else
only make it worse. What is
wrong with those people?"

When class ended, she
handed me a note as she
left the room. "Sorry

I'm such a mess," it
said. "But I still want to go
to Sadie Hawkins

with you Saturday
night. I'm gonna need you to
cheer me up, okay?"

★ ★ ★

When Angela picked
me up that night, Mom was gone
and Dad was watching

Lawrence Welk. He just
waved at me when I told him
I was going out

with some friends. Before
we even got to her car,
Angela stopped, threw

her long arms around
me, and planted a wet kiss
right on my mouth. We

stood in the shadows
of my garage, holding and
kissing like I was

going off to war
the next morning. Then she sighed.
"I needed that, Ashe.

God knows, I really
needed that." She felt soft and
strong and smelled faintly

of cinnamon. I
struggled to steady my voice —
"Happy to oblige" —

and kissed her again.
We finally drove to the
dance but never left

her car. Instead of
dancing, we talked and talked, not
about Vietnam,

civil rights, riots,
or anything else but us:
Angela and Ashe.

After our Sadie's
date, Angela wanted to
meet my family,

but that was the last
thing I wanted. My home life
couldn't take any

more drama. I told
her that my parents were on
the brink of divorce,

so a meet-up was
not a good idea. "But my
mom would love you," I

said, and left it at
that. But Angela's too smart
for that. "What about

your dad?" She smiled. "Would
he love me, too?" Trying to
avoid her eyes, I

shrugged and said, "Well, Dad's
complicated," and changed the
subject. How could I

explain my dad's old-
fashioned attitudes about
war? I didn't want

to risk losing my
girlfriend and my family
both at the same time.

★ ★ ★

At home, raw tension
entangled our lives. Mom's and
Dad's orbits rarely

intersected, and
when they did, they passed in a
silence as cold as

outer space. Most nights,
Dad worked late, Mom attended
protest rallies, and

I'd eat alone, do
my homework, and go to bed
without seeing them.

Sometimes I'd lie in
bed, wondering if things could
have been different.

★　★　★

I came home from school
one day and found my mom in
the kitchen, crying

into the phone. Tears
streaked her red cheeks, and when she
saw me, she wiped her

eyes, turned her back to
me, said, "Gotta go," and hung
up, looking guilty.

I knew she didn't
want to talk about why she
was crying. It was

probably about
Dad, a rally, or something
heavy. I had planned

to tell her about
Angela, but she didn't
need anything else

to worry about,
so I headed upstairs to
tune out. Something was

going on with her,
and I didn't like the tell-
tale signs. She'd shift from

being mellow to
being emotional, and
then ravenously

hungry. Could it be
marijuana? She could buy
it at those rallies

or anywhere on
campus. It was hard to think
my mom had become

a pothead, but who
could blame her? Maybe getting
high helped her deal with

her failed marriage and
all the crap going on in
the world around her.

Angela and I
had our first "disagreement"
over a movie.

She wanted to see
Guess Who's Coming to Dinner,
but I wanted to

see *Bonnie and Clyde,*
and as we argued about
it, I felt myself

acting like my dad.
I stopped. Arguing. Talking.
Looking, listening,

that was better, way
better, and the longer I
looked at her, the less

I cared about what
movie we went to. I just
wanted to be with

her. Standing outside
the theater, watching the
soft curve of her lips

and the light from the
marquee glittering in her
chocolate brown eyes,

I wondered when Dad
stopped feeling this way about
Mom. When did they start

to care more about
ideas than each other? I
took Angela's hand,

pulled her to the box
office, and bought two tickets
to *Guess Who's Coming*

to Dinner. Even
if I had known in advance
that she was going

to cry through the whole
movie, I wouldn't have changed
anything that night.

Angela's parents
welcomed me into their home,
and their kindness stirred

a rush of envy
in me. They appeared to be
everything I'd hoped

my own family
could have been. Mr. Turner,
a political

science professor
at ASU, shook my hand
like we were old friends.

"Angela's told us
a lot about you, so we're
glad to finally

meet the famous Ashe
Douglas." We sat around their
kitchen table and

talked and laughed and ate
peanut butter cookies and
filled the room with a

warmth I'd never known.
But I wrecked it all when I
asked about their son.

"Kelly?" Angela's
mother faded like someone
had punched her off switch.

"He . . ." A panicked look
to her husband, and he slid
his hand over hers,

patting it gently
while he told me they hadn't
heard anything from

Kelly, Angela's
older brother, for a while.
"Army mail isn't

very efficient,
especially coming out
of Vietnam, and

our son's never been
much of a letter writer,
but still, we worry.

When you've got a boy
at war, it's tough not knowing
if he's okay or

not." Angela nudged
me with her foot and nodded
at the door. "I'm sure

he's fine," she said. "But
he should know we need to hear
from him more often."

★ ★ ★

Angela walked me
outside and told me how her
brother's silence had

tied her family
up in knots. "Dad handles it,
but it's killing my

mother. She can't stop
worrying about him, if
he's dead — or worse." When

I wondered what was
worse than dead, Angela said,
"Missing in action."

Seventeen is my

favorite prime number, and

not because I'm a

number nerd. Dad wore

seventeen in college, just

like Dizzy Dean, his

old baseball hero.

I wore it too, of course, but

it wasn't just sports

that made me like it.

When I was young, Mom really

loved a Beatles song

that had the line, "Well,

she was just seventeen, you

know what I mean . . . ," and

I thought it was cool
to hear a song based on my
birthday, and then I

started noticing
seventeens everywhere, and
it made me feel like

I belonged to a
secret club. The Celtics' John
Havlicek wears my

number, and it's the
number of syllables in
a haiku poem,

and it's the day in
May when *Brown versus Board of
Education* was

announced, and it's the
age you can give blood, join the
military, and

get married, and it's
the name of a magazine
for girls, and it's the

number of years a
weird kind of cicada lives
underground before

coming out to mate,
and it's the day I was born,
and for years I'd been

looking forward to
turning seventeen on May
seventeenth. I can't

say for sure what I
expected to happen the
day when my birthday

stars all aligned, but
I figured something special
would take place, something

I'd never forget.
In a way, I felt like that
cicada, and I

was ready to dig
out from underground and get
on with adult life.

★ ★ ★

But my birthday got
off to a lousy start when
I heard on the news

that the past two weeks
were the bloodiest ever.
More than one thousand

Americans died
in Vietnam in those two
weeks, and Angela's

family still had
no word from Kelly, and Mom
was in bed acting

sick the whole time. How
could I celebrate when so
much was going wrong?

When you start to love
someone like Angela, you
learn how to talk and

how to listen, and
you start talking about things
you've never before

dared to say out loud —
all kinds of things: dreams, goals, and
fears. Angela planned

to change the world by
joining the Peace Corps and then
teaching grade school kids.

"If we want to change
things," she said, "that's where we've got
to start." I loved her

confidence, her faith
in the future, and I wished
that I had some of

her rock-solid self-
assurance. I thought a girl
like her feared nothing,

but I was wrong. She
was worried about what might
happen if Kelly

turned out to be a
POW or, worse,
missing in action.

"I don't know if Mom
could take it." Her voice soft now,
edged with dread. "I don't

know if *I* could take
it." She sighed, and a heavy
silence filled the air

between us before
she spoke again. "And sometimes
I'm afraid, just plain

afraid of all the
craziness in the world right
now. There's so much I

want to do, Ashe, but
what if something happens that
blows up all my dreams?"

The ache in her voice
surprised me, and I didn't
know what to say, but

I knew that if I
had to, I'd gladly dive on
a grenade for her.

★ ★ ★

Angela knew that
I was afraid of getting
drafted and sent to

Vietnam. She knew
it wasn't politics that
made me oppose the

war, it was plain old
fear. I can't explain it; I
was as loyal as

the next guy, but the
thought of battle turned my spine
to ice. I didn't

want to die, but I
also worried that in a
life-and-death battle,

my hesitation,
my fear might cause someone else
to die. With bullets

flying and mortar
shells exploding all around,
would I have the guts

to sacrifice my
life to save my buddies? If
a live grenade rolled

into camp, it would
kill me if I covered it
or if I didn't.

In my heart I knew
that if I went to war, I
wouldn't make it back —

or if I did make
it, I'd be in pieces, a
ruined, useless shell.

★ ★ ★

Angela knew my
stupid dream, too. I used to
think that a baby

sister would heal my
family, and I hoped and
prayed that Mom would get

pregnant and that a

new sister would bind all of

us together: two

males, two females: a

perfect balance. "It sounds dumb

now. I realize

my family is

too fractured to be fixed, too

off-kilter to be

balanced, but growing

up, I was desperate for

a little sister."

Angela's eyes turned

soft, and she touched my cheek so

gently I almost

melted. "Be careful

what you wish for, Ashe. Sometimes

girls can create more

problems than they solve."

It turned out she knew what she was talking about.

I'm an idiot.
Mom wasn't smoking dope, though
I almost wish she

had been. I see now,
the symptoms were obvious:
she was *pregnant,* not

stoned. Some guy she met
at an anti-war rally;
she wouldn't tell me

anything about
the man, not even his name.
"Later," she said, "please."

At first I'd assumed
it was Dad, because even
with overwhelming

evidence to the
contrary, I still had my
childish hope that they

might work things out. Well,
they did work things out, but not
how I had hoped. Dad

moved out, furious
at Mom's betrayal, but he
also seemed almost

relieved that he could
leave and blame their failed marriage
on her. When she talked

to me, she didn't
make excuses or try to
explain; she pulled me

into a hug and
whispered over and over,
"I am so sorry."

★　★　★

The last day of school
felt like a wake before an
Irish funeral.

Everybody was
signing yearbooks and talking
about parties and

summer jobs. All the
hallways looked like a whirlwind
had blown through, strewing

crumpled worksheets and
notebook paper everywhere.
Students wandered in

and out of classes
without hall passes because
everyone knew that

summer vacation
had begun even if school
wasn't yet over.

I felt the happy
vibe, too, but bittersweetness
dogged me all morning.

Seeing Angela
turned the bitter to sweet, and
the fog began to

lift. Like everyone
else, I looked forward to our
summer vacation,

but I knew I'd miss
the routine of school. Classes,
homework, sports — it gave

me something to do
besides worrying about
the chaos at home.

★ ★ ★

Before he turned class
over to yearbook signing,
Mr. Ruby told

us he'd be teaching
a new senior course next year,
Contemporary

Civilization,
it would be called, and it would
focus on current

world affairs. He glanced
around the room. "It will be
challenging, even

controversial," he
said, "but I guarantee that
it will be a real

education." His
gaze settled on me when he
said, "I sincerely

hope some of you will
enroll." Angela's pat on
my shoulder confirmed

what I already

knew. When fall rolled around, we'd

both be in that class.

My mom loved Bobby
Kennedy. He stood up for
everything Nixon

didn't, and even
though he couldn't possibly
replace JFK,

he could pick up where
his older brother had left
off when his life was

snuffed out in Dallas
in 1963. When
Bobby entered the

presidential race,
even pregnancy couldn't
slow Mom down. She made

phone calls, wrote letters,
and attended rallies like
it was going to

change the world. A part
of her had died when Martin
Luther King was killed,

but Bobby's campaign
brought it back to life. And it
distracted both of

us, for a time, from
the relentless slaughter in
the Vietnam War.

Wednesday night, Mom and
I watched the California
primary. Bobby

Kennedy won, and
throughout his speech Mom stood and
yelled "Right on!" at the

TV every time
Kennedy made a point she
liked. After the speech,

reporters discussed
the election results and
Kennedy's chances

in November. Then
the TV picture lurched and
rolled, and the people

behind the newsmen
started running and shouting.
Mom froze and stared as

pandemonium
erupted on the TV.
She faded back in-

to her chair, one hand
against her cheek, while she stared
in terrible white

anticipation.

The camera focused on

the swirl of people,

and the reporter

disappeared from sight. Moments

later, a panicked

voice crackled through the

airwaves: "Kennedy's been shot!

My God, he's been shot!"

"It's complicated."
That's what my mom always said
when I asked her when

I'd meet the baby's
father. "Complicated" was
an understatement.

I knew it was the
Age of Aquarius and
free love, but my own

mother, a married
woman, carried the child of
another man. That

was complicated
for everyone involved. Mom's
not stupid, so I

couldn't figure out
how she got pregnant in the
first place. After all

the grief she suffered
from her first pregnancy, she
had to know better,

and given that I
had no siblings, it was clear
that she understood

how birth control worked.
Could she have fallen in love
with some strange peacenik?

Maybe it was just
a desperate one-night stand
that she fell into

out of loneliness.
Maybe she didn't even
know his name. Maybe

he was just drifting
through, and he didn't tell her
where he went next. I

wanted to be mad
at her, to punish her for
putting that last straw

on Dad's back, to make
her pay for lighting the fuse
that would blow up our

fractured family,
but I knew Dad was as much
to blame as she was,

and somehow I felt
that part of the fault was mine,
too. I couldn't be

mad at Mom or Dad
for the complications that
entangled us all.

★ ★ ★

Even with the flak
flying around, Angela
wanted to meet my

parents. She's not like
me that way — conflict is one
thing I avoid, but

she sails in, fearless.
One night, we sat under a
palm tree in her front

yard while I described
my dysfunctional parents.
It didn't faze her.

"Your mom sounds great. I
think I'd get along really
well with her." Then I

told her about my
dad and his old-school views on
politics, civil

rights, and the war. She
laughed. "It will be like *Guess Who's
Coming to Dinner,*

except that I'll be
in Sidney Poitier's role —
the outsider who's

a dad's nightmare." I
couldn't help smiling, and she
knew she'd won. "Okay,"

I said, "I'll see what
I can do." Angela hugged
me, hard, and whispered,

"This'll be a good
thing, Ashe. You'll see." The warmth of
her embrace lingered

all the way to my
front door, but when I opened
it, the sadness at

home swept it right out
of me. I wished life was much
less complicated.

Bobby Kennedy's
murder filled Mom with a new
sense of urgency,

and she turned even
more passionate about the
war, civil rights, and

keeping Nixon out
of the White House. Her work kept
her away from home

a lot, so sometimes
I'd go to Dad's apartment
for dinner. I tried

to talk about the
baby once, but Dad only
stared at me before

leaving the table
without saying a word. I
tried to imagine

a dinner with Mom,
Angela, and him. It was
impossible. I

told Angela that
life isn't like the movies,
and that even if

people need to change,
most don't want to, no matter
what you do or say.

Why don't they publish
all the names of the soldiers
killed every week? How

different it would
be to read a long list of
names in the paper

on Thursdays. It would
bring the war home in a way
numbers can't. Maybe

then people would see
what it's costing us to be
tangled up in a

foreign jungle war
that will get worse before it's
all over. Last week,

one hundred eighty-
seven U.S. soldiers died
in Vietnam, and

nobody — except
family and close friends — knew
or cared. How easy

it is to forget
the blood, injuries, and death
happening daily.

They deserve to be
remembered by name. Think of
what it would be like

to see all the names
of the dead at once. Thousands
of sons, brothers, and

husbands who died for
a country they loved in a
distant, senseless war.

Dad got me a job
digging sprinkler line trenches
for the new hotel

going up over
on Rural Road. My boss was
an old man who had

spent way too much time
in the sun. The first morning,
he laughed when I showed

up without gloves. He
handed me a shovel and
pointed to a guy

already picking
a flat patch of hard brown dirt
in the corner. "Get

busy. I want to
see nothing but backsides and
elbows until lunch.

You got it?" I took
the shovel and walked over
to my coworker.

A dark splotch of sweat
already stained the back of
his gray Marines tee

shirt, and when he saw
me, he swung his pick into
the ground, pulled off his

glove, and shook my hand.
Reuben Ortega was four
years older than me,

and he'd just gotten
back from Vietnam. He lent
me an old pair of

leather work gloves and
shared his ice water while we
broke our backs on the

hard-packed clay in the
broiling July sun. And when
we sat in the shade

of the new building
to eat lunch, he told me things
that he had seen and

done in 'Nam, things that
never make the newspapers.
I was surprised how

calm he was about
the war — and how his stories
haunted me. "It's a

bad scene over there,"
he said. "Real bad." He lit a
cigarette, took a

long drag, and while smoke
drifted upward like a lost
soul, he shook his head.

The summer and Dad
were brutal to Mom. The sun
melted energy

out of her, and she
spent afternoons, the worst part
of every July

day, in the quiet
coolness of her bedroom. Most
days she was far too

wiped out to attend
anti-war demonstrations
or political

meetings. At night she'd
shuffle around the house with
a hand on her huge

belly, as if one
false step might break her open.
Digging ditches all

day wiped me out, too,
but Mom's was a different
kind of weariness.

The baby inside
her made Mom suffer. And so
did Dad by dropping

tons of cold legal
stuff on her as punishment
for being pregnant.

The summer tortured
Angela's family as much
as it tortured mine.

Still no word from her
brother, and the Army did
nothing to help. She'd

take turns with her mom
and dad calling bureaucrats
and writing letters,

but in the end, the
military stonewall won.
The Army knew where

Kelly was stationed,
but they couldn't — or wouldn't —
confirm his status.

When I went to the
Turners' house on Friday night,
the place felt like its

spirit had been ripped
from it. Her parents welcomed
me like always, but

their warm smiles couldn't
camouflage the worry etched
onto their faces,

and even though we
sat at the kitchen table
eating cookies and

chatting, the mood felt
forced, fake, hollow. Angela
grabbed my hand. "Let's walk."

★ ★ ★

Smoky strands of clouds
stretched across the orange-red
western sky, and the

dry heat from the baked
sidewalk warmed the soles of our
shoes as we walked to

Meyer Park. Waves of
sorrow radiated from
Angela, and when

our hands brushed, she clutched
mine and pulled us to a stop.
Her eyes glistened with

tears, and she started
talking, fast, about Kelly,
the war, the riots

and demonstrations,
the murders of Kennedy
and King. "Sometimes I

feel like our world is
drowning in madness and death."
Her eyes pleaded for

comforting, wise words,
but I didn't know what to
say. We stood there in

silence while the last
rays of color faded from
the horizon. Then

she squeezed my hand and
we walked to the park, where we
sat on swings, sharing

the weight of worry
that burdened us. We didn't
know what might still be

coming up the hill
in 1968, but
we swore whatever

happened, we'd face it
together. Sitting there in
the dark, our pinkie

fingers linked, I thanked
God that Angela's life had
intersected mine.

It looked like the war
would never slow down. Reuben
laughed when I asked him

about it. "Ain't no
way, man. The white-collar dudes
sitting in D.C.

aren't the ones bleeding.
They have it their way, this war
will last forever,

and if we run out
of Vietcong to blow up,
they'll find some other

war to keep business
hopping." I didn't want to
believe him, because

I was depending
on my college deferment
to keep me safely

out of the draft through
1973. There
was no way we'd still

be in Vietnam
that long, so I'd graduate
from college and step

into a peaceful
working world. But if we were
still at war, I'd be

instant draft bait, and
that would change everything. I
didn't want to think

about it, but all
afternoon, images of
jungle warfare and

death haunted me. If
Reuben was right, in five years
I might be digging

foxholes and dodging
bullets on the front lines of
a jungle war, and

even in the heat
of the Arizona sun,
a chill shivered me.

"It's the not knowing
that's the worst. Is he rotting
in a Vietcong

prison, or is he
dead?" Angela's voice trembled.
"Why don't they tell us

something, Ashe? They have
to know where he is!" She got
worked up like this when

all the worrying
at home dominoed onto
her. She could hold up

when only her mom
freaked, but when her dad caved, too,
she couldn't handle

it, and she'd call to
tell me to meet her at the
park. Last night a mean

desperation gripped
her, a kind of panic-laced
determination

to do something, to
fix things. When I got there, she
was pacing back and

forth in front of the
swing set; as soon as she saw
me, she unloaded:

the frustration and
pain, anger and sadness. I'd
heard it all before

and knew the best thing
I could do was to listen.
So I sat on a

swing while she paced and
talked and swore and cried. When she
finished, she turned to

me and said, "I'd do
anything to save him, Ashe.
Anything. Even

die." The look on her
face told me she meant it, and
I wondered where that

kind of courage and
love came from. If I were in
her shoes, would I be

willing — would I be
able — to sacrifice my
life for a sibling?

After school, I found
Mom whispering into the
phone in the kitchen,

wiping tears from her
cheeks as she sat hunched at the
table. When she saw

me, she hung up and
dabbed her eyes with a tissue.
"Was that Dad?" I asked.

"A friend." And I knew
she meant *that* guy. "Ashe, there is
something you should know

about . . ." But then the
front door opened, and Dad walked
into the kitchen.

Reading the surprise
on our faces, he said, "I
still own this house, you

know, even if I
don't live here anymore. I
came to pick up a

few things." The shock of
seeing Dad made Mom ready
for a fight. "You could

have called." Dad stared at
her, then at me, and sighed. "I
tried," he said, "but the

line's been busy for
more than an hour." Raw tension
smoldered between them,

a standoff just like
old times, but Dad ended it
by going downstairs.

Taking a deep breath,
Mom rested her head on her
hands. "This is a real

rugged patch for me,
Ashe, and I'm going to need
your help to get through

it." The doorbell rang,
and before I could move, I
heard the door open

and Dad's annoyed voice:
"What do *you* want?" Mom paled and
dropped her hand to her

belly. Angela's
voice: "Is Ashe home?" At my front
door. With my dad. I

got up so fast my
chair crashed onto the floor, but
I arrived too late.

She saw me standing
behind my dad and smiled. "Hey,
Ashe." Dad stepped back, took

a long look at her,
then turned on me. "Who is this?"
Icy slivers spiked

his voice, and I felt
hearts and hopes and doors slamming
shut as I fumbled

for answers that would
satisfy my father and
my hippie girlfriend.

Angela and her
mother brought dinner over
Wednesday night. When she

had heard about Dad,
she insisted on doing
something to help. "Mom

and I know something
about loss," she had said. "And
it's no fun dealing

with it alone." When
they walked in, it felt like they
breathed life back into

our home. Angela's
mom hugged my mother like they
were long-lost sisters,

and Mom's eyes teared up
when she met Angela. "I'm
sorry about what

happened the last time
you came over. Ashe's dad . . .
well, just let me say

I'm sorry, but I
am delighted to meet you."
After eating, we

went downstairs to watch
the evening news, but when a
report on the war

came on, I jumped up
and changed the channel to a
news program about

a massive high-rise
office building project that
was getting started

in New York City.
These twin office towers, said
the reporter, would

be the world's tallest,
a permanent monument
to America's

ingenuity,
capitalistic system,
and democracy.

Mom started laughing.
"Isn't it ironic that
we're bombing the hell

out of one country
while we're building monuments
to our own greatness?"

The room fell silent;
I felt the awkwardness of
Mom's political

statement. But seconds
later Angela's mom said,
"I hear you, sister."

The attention from
Mrs. Turner really helped
my mom get through some

rough days, but still I
worried. Sometimes after work,
I'd find Mom in her

bedroom, panting and
moaning and dripping with sweat.
I'd never felt so

weak and desperate.
If Mom went into labor
at home, what would I

do? What could I do?
Call an ambulance and hope
it would get her to

the hospital in

time? What if something went wrong?

Complications — or

worse? If I lost my

mom, the baby, or both, what

would become of me?

Pounding dirt in the
pounding Arizona sun
darkened my skin and

hardened my body,
and Reuben Ortega made
me appreciate

the broiling heat. "You
think this is tough," he said, "try
a couple days in

a muddy foxhole
with mortar shells dropping all
around you day and

night"—he'd stare into
the distance and his voice would
get ragged—"never

knowing if shrapnel
or a sniper will nail you
while you're sweating in

a stinking hellhole,
just hoping to make it through
the night." Then he'd snap

out of it, focus
his eyes on me, and say, "Don't
never go to war.

If it don't kill you,
it'll break you, and you'll be
digging ditches with

burned-out war vets in
a hundred-ten-degree heat
the rest of your life."

★ ★ ★

Working with Reuben
changed how I read the weekly
casualty reports.

He'd seen buddies shipped
home in body bags. He'd been
splattered by their blood.

He'd heard their panicked
cries and choking death sobs. He'd
lived through the carnage

and knew some of the
four hundred and eight men who
died last week. To me

they were part of an
abstract number, but to him
they were real flesh-and-

blood men sacrificed
on the altar of war. I
tried to make it real,

but to me and most
Americans, the men who
died were just part of

a tragic count that

changed each week. By the end of

the summer, when I

read the casualty

reports, I remembered the

haunted, wounded look

on Reuben's face when

he talked about the war, and

I earnestly hoped

Kelly wasn't part

of the tragic tally of

dead in Vietnam.

The Democrats named
Hubert Humphrey as their man
to face Nixon in

November, but their
convention exposed all the
conflict in the world

today. Protests in
Chicago led to police
violence that seemed

un-American.
Trouble also exploded
in Paris, Prague, and

cities everywhere.
It wasn't just Vietnam;
the world had gone nuts.

* ★ *

The first day of school
felt simultaneously
new and old. Students

jammed the halls, buzzing
and bragging about all their
summer adventures.

My summer had been
a bummer I didn't feel
like sharing at school,

and looking around,
I wondered how many kids
were walking wounded

like me. Our summer
scars didn't show, but the pain
and damage lingered.

Angela met me
at my locker; we held hands
and walked to Mr.

Ruby's room. When he
saw us, he grinned a welcome
and told us to choose

our own seats, so we
claimed the same desks as last year
and waited for class.

"One ninety-five" was
written on the board, and I
knew that his new course,

Contemporary
Civilization, would deal
with today's real life.

My father nagged me
to leave Mom, to move in with
him, but I knew I

couldn't abandon
her, especially so near
to the baby's birth.

He tried bribery,
legal coercion, even
intimidation

to convince me, but
that stuff just shoved us further
and further apart.

I did agree to
meet him for lunch at Pete's Fish
and Chips one Sunday

after school started.
He looked like he hadn't slept
well for a long time.

I got my food, sat
facing him, and prepared to
listen to his pitch.

He made it clear that
reconciliation was
out of the question.

"I know our marriage
was broken, Ashe. Your mother
and I haven't seen

eye to eye on much
of anything since you were
born, but we tried to

hold it together
for your sake." He blinked back tears.
"But this betrayal

is more than I can
bear. She has shamed me and you
and herself, and you

have no idea —
no idea at all — how
much this has wounded

me. I'm going to
fight for you, and I'm going
to make her pay for

what she has done. She
doesn't deserve either one
of us anymore,

and I'll spend my last
dime to make sure that she and
her bastard baby

are completely cut
off. She's made her bed; she can
sleep in it." He leaned

back and stared at me.
"It's going to be scorched earth,
son, no prisoners,

all or nothing — and
you are going to be with
me or against me."

It started late on
Monday night. I heard Mom cry
out in pain. Then she

yelled for me to get
ready to drive her to the
hospital. She'd talked

me through all this in
advance, but something about
it scared the hell out

of me. I checked on
her, then went to the garage,
started the car, and

battled the panic
while I waited. When she got
into the car, pain

sparked off her, and she
panted and sweated like she
was going to melt.

"Should I call someone?"
I asked. She shook her head. "It's
better this way. He'll

find out soon enough.
Now hurry up, unless you
want this baby to

be born in the front
seat." By the time we got to
the emergency

entrance, sweat soaked my
tee shirt, and my hands trembled
like an old man's. They

whisked Mom away, and
I staggered to the waiting
room to worry and

wait. It was after
midnight, so nothing was on
the TV. I leafed

through old magazines
to stay calm, but with every
passing minute, the

worry cranked up a
notch. And then anger started
edging around the

worry. The peacenik
should have been there, not me. He
should have driven Mom

to the hospital
while she twisted and groaned with
labor pains. I stared

at the clock. If I
had known his name and number,
I would have dropped a

dime in the pay phone
and called him to demand that
he come to fix this

mess he started, to
take responsibility
for Mom and their new

baby. But all I
could do was sit and sulk and
worry. Before long,

a nurse walked in. "Ashe
Douglas?" I couldn't read her
face. Was something wrong

with Mom? The baby?
I stood up, and she looked at
me with surprise. "You're

the brother?" Then, "Well,
congratulations. You have
a baby sister."

"Miscegenation,"
the topic of the day in
Mr. Ruby's class.

Arizona had
only recently dropped its
laws against inter-

racial marriage, he
said, but many states still clung
to their old statutes.

Dad was like those states,
still hanging on to racist
traditions and hate.

I slumped in my desk
and shoved those thoughts out of my
head. I didn't want

to deal with it then,

even though it was staring

me right in the face.

Mom named the baby
Rosa, and the first time my
little sister grabbed

my finger with her
tiny hand, she grabbed my heart,
too. Something about

that flooded me with
love, and I was surprised by
the spontaneous

flow of tears that leaked
down my cheeks. She was perfect,
beautiful — and black.

The first time I saw
her, she was still so wrinkled
and baby-new, and

I was so rattled
with relief that she and Mom
had survived birth that

I didn't even
think about her shiny black
hair and beautiful

brown skin. I didn't
even think about what Dad
would say or do. I

didn't even think
about the gossip that would
spread about my mom.

Seeing my baby
sister, my only thoughts were
about how much I

loved her, how I would
always love her, and nothing
anybody said

or did, even Dad,

could change how I felt about

my precious sister.

The very real weight
of responsibility
pressed on me from all

sides after Rosa's
birth. I wanted to fight for
her and Mom, but I

knew the minefield of
divorce would be treacherous,
unpredictable,

and terrifying.
My parents' war paralleled
the violence in

Vietnam, and I
dreaded, truly dreaded that
I might be called on

to fight in both wars
at once. I laugh now when I
remember how I

once believed that a
sweet, innocent baby like
Rosa might mend our

fractured family,
but when Dad finally heard
about her, he swore

he'd ruin Mom and
make sure her black bastard would
rot in foster care.

He must not have known
that when he attacked Mom, I'd
stand in the crossfire.

Thursday, Angela
came over and we watched the
Olympic highlights

while we baby-sat
Rosa for Mom. Sometimes I
think Angela loves

Rosa almost as
much as I do. She calls her
"little soul sister,"

and she always wants
to hold her. Baby Rosa
took to her right off,

and I must admit
that it used to make me feel
kind of jealous to

see Rosa cuddle
up to a stranger more than
she did to me. But

Angela's glow burned
off that jealousy pretty
fast, and it wasn't

long before I loved
how happy my soul sisters
looked with each other.

★ ★ ★

It surprised no one
that American sprinters
Tommie Smith and John

Carlos finished first
and third in the two-hundred
meter; what shocked and

infuriated
people was what they did at
the nationally

televised medal
ceremony. While the "Star
Spangled Banner" played,

both men lowered their
heads and raised black-gloved fists in
a bold Black Power

salute. People booed
and hissed, but the two men took
the abuse in proud,

stony silence. Next
to me, Angela whispered,
"Right on. You look at

that, little girl. Just
look at what those two brothers
are doing for you."

The casualties
over in Vietnam slowed;
the carnage at home

increased. Dad filed for
divorce and hired a big-shot
attorney to sue

for custody. Not
Rosa's, of course. Mine. He claimed
that Mom was unfit

to be my mother,
and he wanted to force me
to live with him and

to leave Rosa and
Mom all alone to fend for
themselves. Mom tried to

hide it from me, but
when I came home from school, she
was sitting in the

living room, Rosa
on her lap, and an opened
letter at her feet.

She'd been crying, but
she sat, still as death, staring
at the letter. "It's

getting nasty, Ashe,
nastier than I thought it
would ever get." Then

her voice caught, and the
tears started again. Rosa
sensed her mom's heartbreak

and started wailing.
I picked up my sister, cooed
and rocked her, and tried

to convince Mom that
everything would be all right.
How, I didn't know.

Dinner with Dad at
Coco's: cheeseburger, fries, a
chocolate shake, and

a huge serving of
quiet. He stared at his plate,
then at me; then he

sighed. Red rimmed his eyes,
and his body sagged like he'd
just finished a long

march through the jungle.
He couldn't sleep anymore,
he said. He missed me,

but after what Mom
had done to him, he couldn't
bear the sight of her.

Dad cleared his throat and
leveled his eyes on mine. I
felt sorry for him

when he said, "I'm just
trying to do the right thing
for you, son. Honest."

★ ★ ★

When I got home, the
peacenik — with a mean Afro,
denim shirt, and bell-

bottoms — sat with Mom
and had Rosa tucked into
the crook of his arm.

He shook my hand, said,
"My name's Marcus," and smiled, but
behind his wire-rim

glasses, his eyes looked
nervous. Rosa's father was
tall, broad-shouldered, and

handsome. Mom said, "You
two should have met sooner. I
should have . . ." She dropped her

eyes. "This wasn't fair
to you — or to Dad — and we
never . . . well, Rosa

was a big surprise.
I'm sorry, Ashe, for what I've
done to our family."

Marcus planted a
gentle kiss on Rosa's head
and handed her to

Mom. "I'll do right by
you and Rosa, but I'm tapped
out and on the run

from the Feds. When I
get settled in Canada,
I'll take care of you."

We believed him, but
in wartime, promises are
as solid as smoke.

★ ★ ★

The only good news
that week came on Halloween.
President Johnson

announced a total
halt to the U.S. bombing
in North Vietnam.

"It's a start," Mom said.
"Maybe it'll turn out to
be the beginning

of the end of the
war. Maybe by the time you
graduate, we'll be

out of Vietnam,
and you won't have to worry
about the draft." Mom

would turn out to be
right, but not in the way that
she and I had hoped.

The optimism
we all felt when LBJ
announced a halt to

the bombing blew up
the next week when Nixon beat
Hubert Humphrey in

the presidential
election. Nixon had made
promises about

what he would do to
end the war, but Mom didn't
believe him. To her,

he didn't seem like
someone the American
people ought to trust.

★ ★ ★

The morning after
the election, Angela
drifted into school

looking fried. When I
asked her if she was okay,
she just ignored me.

I wasn't surprised.
Mom had stayed up late watching
the election news,

and she was so mad
that morning she could hardly
talk. Angela felt

just as strongly as
Mom did, so I thought Nixon
was the reason for

her grave mood. We walked
to Mr. Ruby's class in
silence, and before

we reached the door, she
pulled me into a fierce hug
and started bawling.

The Army, she said,
had just sent news about her
brother: MIA.

I didn't know what
to do or say, so I just
stood there and held her

while she quietly
sobbed into my shoulder, and
for some reason I

thought about my mom
and dad and Rosa and the
brewing battle that

would tear us apart,
and I started crying, too,
because we had both

lost someone we loved

to a senseless war that could

have been prevented.

Part of the divorce
wrangling included a court
order to appear

before a judge for
a custody hearing. Mom
showed me the papers

during dinner while
she was nursing Rosa. "I
don't want to lose you,"

she said tenderly,
and I wasn't sure if she
meant me or Rosa,

but as I watched my
baby sister snuggled with
Mom, I knew what she

had meant. I couldn't
blame her. I was seventeen,
and I could handle

whatever crap Dad
threw at me, but Rosa was
only a baby

who still needed her
mother to love and care for
her. I'd had my turn

being raised by Mom,
and now Rosa should have hers.
I *had* to find a

way I could be a
hero for Rosa in the
coming war with Dad.

Angela gave me
a copper MIA wrist-
band with her brother's

name and the date he
went missing on it. I was
supposed to wear it

until he came home —
or until his body was
found. I slid the smooth

bracelet over my
wrist and wished I had something
to give her, something

permanent like this
wristband that would remind her
of me if I went

missing in action.
Last night, Mom had talked about
running away from

Dad and the hearing,
taking me and Rosa to
California or

Florida or some-
place Dad wouldn't be able
to find us. I tried

to imagine the
three of us living away
from home and friends and

trying to pay the
bills. It wouldn't work, I said.
There's no way we could

earn enough money
to live on *and* pay out-of-
state tuition: the

draft would snatch me on
my next birthday. Mom looked heart-
broken. "What else can

I do? Marcus will
send us whatever money
he can and join us

when we get settled
somewhere." I believed her, but
who'd pay for college?

We ate Thanksgiving
dinner at Angela's house.
Somehow, her mom had

the energy to
host a big meal despite all
their worries about

Kelly. Their home felt
so cozy that Mom and I
lingered long after

dinner. Sharing the
holiday together did
something for both our

broken families,
so when Angela's dad asked
us to celebrate

Christmas with them next
month, Mom and I agreed right
away. The warmth from

Angela and her
parents filled the room, and we
floated home on it.

★ ★ ★

Mom gasped when she saw
Dad's car parked in front of our
house. I steered into

the driveway and shut
off the engine. Mom looked mad —
or scared — and tightened

her grip on Rosa,
who had started to cry. "Take
Rosa inside," I

said. "I'll deal with Dad."
While they left, I got out of
the car and met him

in the front yard. He
reeked of beer. "Is that the black
bastard?" "Rosa," I

said. "My sister's name
is Rosa." I sounded a
hundred times calmer

than I felt. A flash
of pain twisted Dad's face. "How
can you consider

her a sister? Do
you know what your mother did
to me? To *us?*" He

stepped closer. "Come on,
Ashe. I can take you away
from all this right now."

"One ninety-two" was
on the board, and beneath it,
Mr. Ruby wrote

"30,000." He
took a deep breath and told us
that this week, the death

toll in Vietnam
since 1961 hit
that number. He snapped

his fingers. "That's half
of all the residents of
Tempe. Dead." He snapped

his fingers again.
"Gone. The loss is crushing, but
it doesn't even

include civilians,
POWs, or those
missing in action —

and we can't even
begin to calculate what
we've suffered at home."

I thought about those
weekly casualty counts,
the stern mug shots of

local guys killed in
action, Kelly MIA,
and the trauma in

my own home. Mr.
Ruby really knew what he
was talking about.

Last week, two letters
dropped on our house like mortar
shells. The first announced

that a judge would soon
end our financial support
from Dad. Rosa and

Mom would be cut off
forever; me, too — unless
I lived with my dad.

Abandon Rosa
and Mom, and he'd pay all my
college expenses,

thus guaranteeing
a four-year draft deferment.
Stay with Mom and lose

everything. Dad's threat
burned me, but Mom stayed cool. "We
can count on Marcus,"

she said. "It won't be
easy, but he'll send enough
for us to get by."

Her tightlipped smile showed
her determination to
keep this part of our

family intact.
She opened the next letter,
and while she scanned the

page, her hand trembled,
and her determined façade
faded. She dropped the

letter and grabbed me
like she was drowning. "Marcus
is dead," she whispered.

Angela cried when
she heard, and worry spilled out
with her tears. "What are

you going to do,
Ashe? What are you going to
do?" She hugged me and

wouldn't let go. Mom
worried, too, when I said I'd
quit school and get a

job. "That's crazy! What
about college? Live with your
dad — something will work

out for us." Her words
dripped with doubt. Dad had tossed a
grenade into our

family, and Mom
wanted to be the hero.
I couldn't let her;

I couldn't live with
Dad while Mom and Rosa were
dumped on the street. He

had us trapped, and
I had to figure out the
answer. Angela

and I stayed up late
talking about options, and
though she wouldn't say

it, there was only
one that might work, one she and
I couldn't discuss.

Christmas brought no gifts
except time, plenty of time
for thinking about

what heroes do. I
figured out that a hero
is someone who risks

his life for something
greater than himself. Throughout
history, people

have accepted risks
for some greater good, and I
could think of nothing

greater than the well-
being of Mom and Rosa.
I loved them more than

I hated war — and
even more than I feared death.
It was my turn to

sacrifice. When she
found out, Angela pounded
my chest, then collapsed

into me, sobbing.
She agreed to meet at the
Greyhound bus depot

to say goodbye and
swore she would keep my secret
until I was gone.

★ ★ ★

Waiting for the bus,
we sat on a wooden bench
holding hands, talking,

and kissing like there
was no tomorrow — and I
learned that mourning starts

with goodbye. When I
stood to leave, I gave her my
MIA bracelet.

My DI at Fort
Polk loved to say, "Boot camp will
make men out of boys,"

but he really meant
that boot camp turns hearts of flesh
into hearts of stone.

You can't kill if you
feel. For eight grueling weeks, we
ran, climbed, crawled, fought, fired,

and ran some more on
little food and less sleep. I
dropped into my bunk

each night like a dead
man, only to be rousted
before the sun cracked

the horizon, and
except for five minutes a
week, I had neither

the energy nor
the time to write letters home
or think anything

but what the Army
expected me to think. I
graduated and

posed for my Army
photograph, staring like I
was dead serious.

I belong to the
101st Airborne now,
and our CO said

we should all buy life
insurance, so I did, and
before I deployed,

I made sure my pay
goes to Mom — and if I don't
make it, she'll get the

insurance, too. A
humid hell is my home now,
with death lurking in

jungle shadows. I
flinch at everything, and my
M16's always

ready to kill. On

night patrols, two things keep me

going: survival

and the people I

love. I dream of Rosa, Mom,

Angela — even

Dad — and wonder if

they're looking at this same moon,

thinking about me.

Hill 937

Dug in, waiting for
Operation Apache
Snow to launch. My fox-

hole feels too shallow.
I can't stop the sweats and shakes:
Am I sick — or scared?

If you can't read this,
it's because I am writing
it in a hurry.

I see Death coming
up the hill, and I am not
ready to meet him.

HISTORICAL NOTE

The last two stanzas of this book are based on an American soldier's letter written shortly before he died in the assault on Hamburger Hill in May 1969. His letter appeared as part of an article, "One Week's Dead," published in *Life* magazine on June 27, 1969. The full text can be viewed online: http://life.time.com/history/faces-of-the-amercan-dead-in-vietnam-one-weeks-toll/#1.

The official death toll for U.S. soldiers in Vietnam in 1968 is 16,592. If you're a numbers person, you'll notice that the sum of the weekly death counts Ashe reads in the newspapers is something less than 16,592. Here's why:

1. By 1968, the war in Vietnam was extremely unpopular, so it's likely that the weekly press releases underreported the dead to minimize the tragic consequences of our involvement in Southeast Asia.

2. Even if military leaders wanted an accurate weekly death count, tallying the numbers was difficult because of the nature of the war. Some units in distant parts of Vietnam simply may

not have been able to submit their reports on time — or at all.

3. MIAs were not counted as dead until their bodies were recovered and identified, a process that could take more than a year.

4. In the chaos of war, even a dedicated clerk made mistakes. Such mistakes probably would not have been caught before the weekly report was announced.

There is no database that lists the 1968 casualties by week, so I did what Ashe would have done: I reviewed the Thursday edition of daily newspapers for each week's death count. The numbers that head each chapter are the numbers reported in newspapers in the fifty-two weeks that comprised 1968.

AUTHOR'S NOTE

When historical novelist Gary D. Schmidt visited my classes at BYU in 2010, he mentioned that more U.S. soldiers died in 1968 than in any other year of the Vietnam

War. A year later, I started working on a novel set in 1968 and decided to see if Schmidt had been right. It turned out he was: 16,592 American soldiers died in 1968. As I began digging into the history, I also learned that the weekly casualty reports appeared in newspapers each Thursday, but by 1968, the reports had become so commonplace that many Americans barely noticed them. I wanted my main character to notice and become fascinated by the death counts as he gained an awareness of the troubled world around him.

I started writing the novel in prose, but after a few chapters, the project stalled. Rather than give up, I tinkered with the prose, with the point of view, with the character's voice, but nothing seemed to help. In an early draft, I had enjoyed inserting historical information like Ashe's birthday, May 17, 1954, the date of the U.S. Supreme Court decision *Brown v. Board of Education,* and that's when the prime number 17 started growing on me, so I looked for other opportunities to plant the number into the story. Playing with numbers was fun for a while, but it soon became clear that no amount of number play would revive my manuscript.

During this period of writer's block, I woke up early

one morning with the story on my mind, and as I lay in bed, I started thinking about the number 17 and the other numbers that appeared in the story and wondered how I might use them. What else relied on 17? Well, haiku has 17 syllables; maybe I could have my character write haiku as a hobby. Or maybe I could divide the book into 17 sections and have a haiku introduce each section. What else? Was 1968 divisible by 17? It'd be cool if it was. The 1968 death toll, 16,592, was a big number, and I wondered if it might be divisible by 17. I rolled out of bed, found a calculator, and punched in the numbers. Guess what? The number 1968 isn't evenly divisible by 17, but 16,592 is: 16,592 divided by 17 equals 976.

Then a jolt of creative surprise shook me. What if I wrote the novel entirely in haiku? What if the novel contained one syllable for every U.S. soldier who died in 1968? What if the entire story were contained by a syllable count? It sounded crazy. It sounded like a stupid gimmick. It sounded impossible. But I decided to try it anyway.

The novel took off. Of course, the format was maddening, and revision was incredibly complicated. I soon learned that when your writing is bound up in clusters of 17 syllables arranged in lines of five, seven, and five, a single word change ripples forward and backward and causes much more rewriting and wordsmithing than I could have imagined.

The number 17 had one more surprise for me. Without my planning it, that prime number came into play in the book's final scene. I wanted Ashe to be writing about 1968 in retrospect and decided to do some research to find out what had been the bloodiest week in Vietnam in 1969. It was the battle of Hamburger Hill, a few days in the middle of May. Somehow it seemed fitting to end Ashe's story there, but it wasn't until the umpteenth revision that I discovered that by using Hamburger Hill as the concluding event, I had Ashe's story end on his 18th birthday: May 17, 1969. It seemed like a fitting way to bring his story and the number 17 full circle.

ACKNOWLEDGMENTS

I'm grateful to many people for this book. First, to the men and women who served their country during the Vietnam era in a horrendous war, and to the families that supported them. Next to the historians who documented not only the war but also everything else that rocked the world in 1968. My agent, Patricia J. Campbell, encouraged me to try the prose-to-haiku revision, and after reading a few chapters, she pressed me to take it further. Christy Hughes provided a careful and very smart read of an early version of the manuscript and offered detailed suggestions for revision that proved helpful in rewriting the manuscript. Dr. Jesse Crisler read through the first full draft and gave me suggestions on historical details that reshaped my revisions. John H. Ritter read a near-final copy of the manuscript and offered wisdom and feedback that helped me fine-tune the story. My editor, Karen Grove, took a gamble on this story and its format and helped me reshape the novel and stick to the 17-syllable, five-seven-five stanza consistently from start to finish. Finally, I must thank my wife and best friend, Elizabeth, the new girl who showed up in one of my high school classes in 1969 and who has changed my life for the better ever since.